David Dupree
Predicts a Plot

Second in the Egmont School Series

S K Sheridan

For Jan and Dewi

Monday, 1st November

Back again, Diary!

Well I can't tell you how PLEASED I am to be back at Egmont, it's really starting to feel like home now that I've been here for half a term. But it was *so* nice to see my old nanny Carrie Whepple over the half term holiday, I *do* miss seeing her every day. At least I got to see her for a whole week, she moved into our mansion to look after me just like old times, and her achy joints weren't nearly as bad as usual.

My parents had given her loads of money before they disappeared off on yet another Secret Service mission, so we went to the theatre every day, followed by tea and scones in Carrie's favourite café, The Boiled Egg. We even went to see an art show. All the paintings were by someone called Frida Kahlo who seemed to like painting portraits of herself, which Carrie kept tutting about, saying things like, "Wouldn't hurt her to paint a landscape, bit vain if you ask me". Frida Kahlo's eyebrows were so thick they joined together in the middle and I simply couldn't stop looking at them, although she did paint some pretty patterns and use nice bright colours too.

Lessons don't start till tomorrow, so me and Arabella spent our first day back in the swimming pool. Lots of splashing.com! We'd been surfing on our tummies while the wave machine was on, and were just climbing on to a floating, plastic castle, when who should appear but Cleo and Clarice. They don't like getting their hair wet so they were both wearing jewel studded bathing hats and looked a bit over dressed.com for swimming, even if we *are* in a luxury boarding school. They walked slowly to the edge of the pool, dipped their toes in, shivered, then went and sat in the hot, bubbling Jacuzzi.

'Oh look, it's the nerd brains,' Clarice called when she spotted Arabella and me. 'Trying to learn how to doggy paddle and not sink like stones, are we girls?'

'Just ignore them,' Arabella whispered. 'At least they're too wimpy to come near us in the proper pool.'

'Are either of you thinking of auditioning for the school play?' Cleo yelled. 'Not that you have the faces for the stage of course, we wouldn't want the audience to be frightened away. Unlike Clarice and

I, who will *definitely* be auditioning, won't we?' Clarice nodded, smoothing down her bathing hat as tons of bubbles rose up around her.

'Actually we're BOTH thinking of auditioning, aren't we Davina?' Arabella called back over the echoey noise of the swimming pool. She scrambled on to the pink floating castle and stood up, her red curls all frizzy. Oh no, I really wish she wouldn't do this. Whenever Cleo or Clarice annoy her she always rises to the challenge, gets cross and we end up in a sticky situation.

'Um, are we?' I said vaguely, also trying to clamber on to the slippery castle.

'Yes, don't you remember, we were talking about it this morning?' Arabella looked down and waggled her eyebrows. I sighed and nodded as I gripped the sides and pulled myself on, my long brown plait stuck to my back.

Cleo and Clarice went into huge belly aches of laughter, rotten things.

'You two, on the stage?' Clarice laughed so hard her jewelled bathing hat wobbled half off. 'Now that would be HILARIOUS!'

Arabella was just about to say something back, I *do* wish she would keep her temper around those bullies, when the dolphin shaped door to the swimming pool opened and Mrs Pumpernickle, our housemistress, bustled in with two new girls behind her. One was pale and wore glasses and had chin length dark brown hair. She looked up at the multi coloured swimming slides that snake in and out above the pool, blinking. The other girl looked bored, had a white fur coat tied round her tubby belly and bronze curls that cascaded down to her waist.

'The swimming pool at our villa in Italy is much better than this one, it has gold statues of lions at each of its corners and a silver slide going from the pool to the ocean. This pool looks a bit boring,' said the girl wearing the white fur coat. Well! What a rude thing to say on your first day. I saw Cleo and Clarice giving her evil stares over the edge of the Jacuzzi and for once I didn't blame them.

Mrs Pumpernickle rolled her eyes, as though she'd heard one too many comments like that from the new girl but was too polite to say anything. She ushered the girls nearer to the side of the pool.

'This is Lottie Greenwood and Erica Anchor. They'll both be in Sapphire class and I know you'll make them feel welcome while they get to know their way around.' Mrs Pumpernickle looked at me and Arabella and then glared at Cleo and Clarice, who'd slid down in the Jacuzzi so only the tops of their heads were showing. I smiled at the scared looking girl who I think was Lottie, after all I know what it feels like to be new, I've only been at Egmont Exclusive Boarding School myself for a few weeks. She pushed her glasses up her nose and gave me a small grin. The other girl, Erica, just stared at the wall. Hmm, not quite sure what to make of her.

We're back in our dorm now, dry and warm. This term we have pale blue duvets with moons and stars all over them that actually light up when you press a switch at the side. So magical.com. I've just been drying my hair with Arabella's hairdryer. My hair's now down to my bottom, the longest I've ever had it. Carrie says I need it trimmed, but I like it like this, it keeps my back warm in the cold weather.

'Are you serious about us auditioning for the school play?' I asked Arabella, hoping that she wasn't, unplugging her purple and green spotty hairdryer.

'Yes, absolutely,' she swung round to face me, her eyes looking all fiery. 'I mean, can you imagine if Clarice and Cleo get the main parts? It would be AWFUL. I don't think I'd be able to watch even five minutes of the show, they'd be preening and posing, it would make me want to be SICK. We definitely have to audition and I'm going to ask the rest of Sapphires to do so as well, just so that pair of conceited so and so's have some healthy competition.'

'Alright, calm down,' I said, grinning. 'That's fine but I have to warn you, I've never done any acting before, so I'll probably be pretty rubbish.'

Mmm, some delicious smells are wafting under the door, it must be dinner time. Ooh, I wonder what delights Marcel and his team of chefs have for us tonight...

Tuesday 2nd November

The excitement mounts, Diary...

So last night, Arabella and I ended up sitting at the same table as the new girls, Lottie and Erica. Lottie is a bit of a sweetie, she's here on a Maths scholarship so must be pretty clever. She said her parents could never afford to send her to Egmont without the scholarship and because she passed loads of difficult maths tests she'll now get all her school fees paid. She said her family only own one, three bedroom house and one quite old car. My parents have loads of cars but I didn't say that because I didn't want to make her feel bad. Anyway, I don't know *why* my parents have so many cars or houses, they're never around to enjoy them because they're always off on some secret spy mission, so what's the point?

The nasty girls Cleo and Clarice just HAD to come and say mean things when they found out Lottie was here on a scholarship.

'Oh you're a *poor* girl are you?' Cleo sneered, leaning on our table and swishing her blonde hair in Lottie's face. 'How interesting, I've never met anyone poor before.'

'The school's standard must be dropping if they're letting riff raff in now,' Clarice said, looking down her nose at Lottie, who gulped and looked at the table cloth.

'Cleo, Clarice, what on *earth* are you doing out of your seats?' Mrs Pumpernickle came bustling along, frowning. 'Go and sit down at once. What an awful example you're setting to the new girls, such bad manners.' Cleo and Clarice nudged each other and sniggered, before sashaying off.

'Don't listen to them, Lottie,' Arabella said. Her cheeks had gone red so I knew she was angry.

'They're mean to everyone. They like to find people's weak spots, it's really pathetic. You should have seen how they treated Davina and I last term when we were campaigning to be prefects.'

'I do find everything here a bit scary actually,' Lottie said, tears coming into her eyes. 'Including them. Everything is so big and expensive looking, there's even a menu at dinner time. At home we usually have beans on toast, or sausages and mash. I mean look,' she held up the menu. 'Tonight we can order caviar on bruschetta to start with and I don't even know what that is.' A tear rolled down her cheek and I went to give her a hug.

'Caviar is just fish eggs, they look small and black, and bruschetta is like crunchy bread. Try it, it's a rather tangy combination,' Arabella grinned. 'Don't worry, you'll soon get used to all the glitz and glamour and you'll probably find that most people here are nice and normal, even if they have got more money than you're used to. It's only a handful of people like Cleo and Clarice who are unbearable snobs.'

Hmm, I thought, looking at Erica, who as usual was looking bored. She might just fall into the unbearable snob category.

'Erica, what school did you go to before you came to Egmont?' I asked, giving her my biggest smile. I wondered if I'd got her wrong and she just looked bored by accident, when she was actually nervous or something. Don't judge a book by its cover, Carrie always says.

'I had a full time governess,' Erica said, yawning. 'My father paid through the nose for the best teacher he could find to come and live with us. She taught me all the subjects like maths, writing, history, geography, art and music. I'm extremely clever, my governess told me that all the time, so I'll probably find all the work here at Egmont really easy and rather dull.'

Arabella laughed then turned it in to a cough. Lottie looked down at the tablecloth again, looking even more depressed than before. I stared at Erica, wondering why anyone would actually *announce* that they were clever. Surely Lottie was clever if she got a Maths scholarship, but she didn't go on about it like that. In fact she didn't seem to have much confidence in herself at all.

Just then, a loud crash rang through the dining room. The two metal kitchen doors swung on their hinges, and about twenty chefs wearing puffy white hats and black and white checked trousers burst into the hall. In the lead was Marcel, our tiny, French head chef.

'Uh oh, here we go,' Arabella said. She looked at me and grinned, then leaned towards Lottie and Erica. 'You'll get used to this, they do it every evening. They seem a bit crazy at first but boy, do they cook good food.'

'Good evening Egmont girls. Marcel and 'iz team are 'ere to take your orders,' the head chef shouted. Then he turned and waved his fist at the larger man behind him. 'You, Jean Paul, you just trod on my foot and 'urt it very much. Say you're sorry right *now*.'

'Never!' The man shouted back. 'Your giant, clod hopping foot was in *my* way. Now let me pass, Marcel, so I can take these poor, starving girls' orders.'

'You 'orrible man, Jean Paul,' Marcel hissed, as he hopped up and down, rubbing his foot. 'Fine, don't say sorry to me. Maybe I will just fire you next week.' With that, each chef ran to a different table, notepads held high. Lottie's mouth was open and even Erica had woken up a bit.

'That was so funny,' Lottie breathed.

'That was ridiculous,' Erica snorted. 'My dad's chef is much more sophisticated than that, he'd never make such a show of himself in public.'

'Let's order,' I said quickly, seeing Arabella grind her teeth. Me and Lottie ordered the cous cous on rye bread to start with, followed by roast chicken, sweet potato mash and peas with triple chocolate cake for dessert. Arabella and Erica asked for the caviar on bruschetta, beef wellington and strawberry surprise and we all ordered cherry and apple cocktails to drink.

After dinner, which was UTTERLY DELISH.COM, Mrs Fairchild stood up and started singing. As usual, she'd been seated at the large, round table in the middle of the dining hall with all the other teachers. I love the tweety canaries that hang in cages above each table, but have never quite got used to the hanging garden above Mrs Fairchild's table, where peacocks strut about in a massive white gold cage, showing off their colourful tail feathers. SO unusual.com.

'Why is she singing?' Erica sighed.

'Because she's lovely and a bit mad,' I said before Arabella could open her mouth. I could tell Arabella had already taken against Erica and to be honest I wasn't that impressed myself, but there didn't seem any point in arguing with the new girl, especially as we don't know her properly. 'Mrs Fairchild always sings and twirls, it makes life more interesting. Sometimes she does yoga in her study and last term she was taking salsa dancing lessons. She really is amazing for someone her age, but don't be fooled, underneath that dizzy smile is a brain as sharp as a razor. Arabella and I found that out before half term when we were in a spot of bother.'

Before Erica could ask what the bother had been about, Mrs Fairchild stopped trilling and said,

'Good evening and welcome back to Egmont, my darling girls. I hope each and every one of you had a good half term. Helicopter and jet drop off was a *little* more organised than last time, but please do remind your parents to steer clear of the flower beds to the south of the hockey pitch. Someone's helicopter landed on them this afternoon and the gardener was so upset I had to give him the rest of the day off.' She stopped and gave a little chuckle. Lottie looked at me with wide eyes, so I leaned towards her and whispered,

'Most girls here get dropped off by helicopter or private jet, although there's a few that come by train, car and taxi.'

'My mum drove me here in her Vauxhall Astra,' Lottie said, looking pale.

'As you know,' Mrs Fairchild went on, her eyes staring at each pupil in turn, suddenly looking less amused and more piercing. 'This term is going to be an extra exciting one because the first years are going to be putting on a fantastic play with the help of Hollywood director, Alfie Calpone, and singing and dancing coach Stephania Sellwig. It will be a chance for their artistic talents to shine, not just on the stage but also off it, helping to prepare the scenery, props and general production.'

Lottie leaned towards me and whispered,

'First years? In my old school we were called Year Sevens.'

'Mrs De Nero our drama teacher will welcome Alfie and Stephania when they arrive at our school tomorrow afternoon,' Mrs Fairchild said, beginning to dance the foxtrot as a murmur of excitement went round the dining hall. Cleo and Clarice immediately snapped open their pocket mirrors and began inspecting their faces before getting out their pocket hairbrushes. Honestly, they're so vain. It's not like that director will whisk them off to Hollywood or anything, is it? 'And I trust you will also make them feel welcome and above all, learn from their expertise.' Mrs Fairchild stopped talking and twirled on the spot until the excited chatter had died down.

'A quick word of warning.' She went on. 'These two highly trained professionals have argued quite publically in the past, but I'm assured that now they are able to work together calmly which is good because they are the best in the business, so really hope the play will come together peacefully and harmoniously.

Just one last thing,' she said as Cleo and Clarice sighed loudly and pretended to be asleep, rude girls. 'Several first years' mothers have kindly offered to stay with us from now until the end of the play, to help make some sensational costumes, so I would like you to welcome them to our school please.' Everyone clapped.

I looked round and saw a table full of mothers absolutely CAKED in makeup, wearing expensive suits, with brightly painted nails on the ends of their fingers that clasped fluted wine glasses. There was one small girl sitting next to the woman at the end, who had her finger up her nose.

'That's Hippolyta, Clarice's little sister,' Arabella whispered loudly. 'She must have come with her mum, Mrs Blinkham. Obviously as charming as her big sis.'

'We call her *Polly* for short, not Hippolyta,' Clarice, who'd overheard, hissed at Arabella.

So now we're back in our dorm after a day of lessons, doing some homework, although I can't really concentrate. Alfie Calpone and Stephania Sellwig are supposed to be arriving in a little while and...well...it's exciting! I've never met anyone famous before...

Wednesday 3rd November

Oh. My. Goodness. Diary!

Never in all my life have I EVER seen such a fuss and commotion as when Alfie and Stephania arrived yesterday. Never!

Oh for goodness sake, where do I start? Well, I was just finishing a history essay about Henry the Eighth, he was certainly a THOROUGHLY UNPLEASANT king, when all this screaming started outside. At first I wondered if Mrs Fairchild had bumped into someone in her Rolls Royce (she's not a very good driver and has flattened the gardener's prize roses twice) but then I heard chants of, "Alfie, Alfie", through the screaming.

Arabella and I literally pelted out of our dorm, along the corridors and out of the massive front doors to find complete chaos in front of us. There was a sea of Egmont girls dressed in glittery pink and white uniforms, bobbing around six long, black shiny cars that had pulled up in the crescent drive.

Cleo and Clarice were suctioned to the sides of the first car like leeches and it was them screaming, "Alfie, Alfie". Someone inside the car was trying to get the door open but they couldn't because Clarice's body was blocking it. In the end the head girl, sixth former Rosalie Arbunkle, who was looking a bit flushed herself, had to peel Clarice away from the car like a banana skin and drag her over to one side.

The door crashed open and a small man who seemed to be made entirely of round, polished curves, got out. He was bald on top except for a fringe of hair round the base of his head and wore an expression like Carrie's friend's pug dog – sort of jowly and displeased.

'That's him,' Arabella whispered. 'That's Alfie Calpone. He looks shorter in real life.'

'Yeah, yeah, hello to you all and all that,' Alfie shouted, eyebrows lowered, no trace of a smile. His voice was deep and rough, as though he'd just eaten a ton of gravel. 'Now can someone tell me where I can get a drink around here? And can you girls move out of my way so my people can unpack my luggage? We need some space so move back will you.' Well! How incredibly unappealing.com. It's a good thing Carrie's not here or she'd have given him a loud piece of her mind for arriving like that, famous or not.

At that moment our drama teacher, Mrs De Nero, came floating round the corner. Mrs De Nero reminds me of a human butterfly, she has long, wavy white hair that wafts out behind her wherever she goes, and she always wears loose, patterned scarves, tops and trousers that seem to flap like butterfly wings when she moves. She went up and kissed the unsmiling Alfie on both cheeks then escorted him off to his luxury, guest apartment, while his 'people' dragged suitcase after suitcase out of the six cars.

'Is he moving in forever?' I whispered to Arabella in wonder and she grinned back, shrugging. How can anyone have that much stuff? Some of the cases and bags were labelled with stickers that read, "Alfie's make up", "Twenty different flavours of tea for Alfie", "Alfie's yoga mat", "Alfie's favourite pillow" and "Alfie's hair dye".

'Didn't think he had much hair left to dye,' Arabella said, nudging me.

The crowd was breaking up, with Cleo and Clarice looking offended, probably because Alfie hadn't recognised their Hollywood potential in the few moments they were lying across his car, when there was a tinkling sound and a bike came zooming down the drive.

'Is that Stephania Sellwig?' I asked, squinting.

'Yes I think so,' Arabella said, as the tall, graceful lady dismounted and removed one, small backpack from her bike. 'She looks much more normal than that Alfie chap, don't you think?'

'Hello girls,' Stephania said in a lilting voice as she swept towards the front door, golden hair wound round her head in an intricate plait. 'It's *so* lovely to meet you, I can't *wait* to see what talents you all have when we start the auditions tomorrow. Your teacher, Mrs De Nero, sent me an email saying to come and find her when I got here, so I'll go in search of her now. See you soon.' And with that she hopped inside and disappeared, Cleo and Clarice following her like two little puppies.

So now we've got lessons all morning and auditions all afternoon. Aggghh! I've never acted in front of anyone in my life and Arabella is absolutely insistent that we both audition, just to annoy the bullies if nothing else. Oh WHAT am I going to do?

Thursday 4th November

Surprising news, Diary.

Yesterday afternoon I felt like digging a hole and sitting in it quietly until the auditions were over, but Arabella didn't let me. Honestly, she's *such* a fiery red head! She came and found me in the library, where I was trying to hide from her behind the biggest stack of books, unsuccessful plan.com, and frog-marched me to the Grand Hall.

I had to admit the hall was looking utterly fabulous. Apparently Mrs Fairchild had hired a team of professional designers over the half term, who'd completely transformed the hall from somewhere we have assemblies and sit exams to a West End standard theatre. It now has a proper high stage with a drop down red curtain, stacks of blank scenery leaning up against the back wall that has to be painted by us pupils, loads of boxes of props and even a trap door in the stage floor. Wowzers.com. The designers even put new rows of seating in. soft red chairs that step up higher and higher towards the ceiling, with pairs of red binoculars for the seats far from the stage. *So* cool.com.

Alfie and Stephania were sitting several seats apart from one another on the front row and Mrs De Nero was perched on the side of the stage. Melody was reading from a script when we got there. She's really good at acting and she wants to be a famous actress when she grows up so I hope she gets a good part.

I saw a whole pile of scripts on one of the seats and the sight of them made me want to be sick. They were titled, "A Midsummer Night's Dream". Arabella stepped forward and grabbed a couple, shoved one at me, then thumbed through the pages of hers excitedly. I couldn't look at mine as I was trying not to faint.

'I don't even know what "A Midsummer Night's Dream" is about,' I muttered.

'All I know is it's by the playwright William Shakespeare. Don't worry, they're bound to explain it to us when rehearsals start,' Arabella said over her shoulder.

There were only two first years ahead of us in the audition queue, and of course it had to be Cleo and Clarice. Clarice's mum, Mrs Blinkham was also there, dolloping bright red LIPSTICK (for goodness sake!) on to her daughter's face.

'Speak clearly, darling,' I heard her whisper loudly. 'Alfie's bound to recognise your star quality if you draw enough attention to yourself.' Hah! Clarice's little sister, Polly, was galloping along rows of seats, pretending to be a horse, stopping to pick her nose every now and again. I didn't see Mrs Blinkham look at Polly ONCE the whole time we were in the Grand Hall, she seemed too busy worrying about getting Clarice a one way ticket to Hollywood. Honestly, that little girl could run out of the hall and her mother wouldn't even notice.

When Melody had finished her turn, Cleo climbed up onto the stage and read her script very quietly, mumbling into her sleeve.

'Not such a big shot now, is she?' Arabella whispered with glee.

Then it was Clarice's turn, her mother fussing over her all the way to the stage. Even though Arabella would never admit it, Clarice was actually quite good. She was playing the part of Helena, who was apparently in love with someone called Demetrius. She read the words confidently and even got carried away and did some actions. When she'd finished to ecstatic applause from her mother, Alfie called out,

'Who's next?' I was nearly sick, thinking it might be me, but then...

'Oh me, me, me!' Arabella ran to the stage and jumped up. She then COMPLETELY astonished me by putting on the most marvellous acting performance I've ever seen. Honestly, she was no longer Arabella, but BECAME someone called Hermia, who was apparently in love with a bloke called Lysander. It seemed like Hermia's dad wanted her to marry Demetrius not Lysander, but I could tell from Arabella's acting that Hermia REALLY didn't want to.

By the time she'd finished, Stephania was on her feet clapping, and even Alfie had a half smile on his face. Cleo, Clarice and Mrs Blinkham, however, had twisted up faces like they'd been sucking on a batch of very strong lemons.

'You were much better than her, darling,' Mrs Blinkham said loudly to Clarice. Yeah right, I thought. Not likely. I walked up to the stage, plucking up my courage, because I'd just had an idea.

'Wasn't Arabella amazing?' I said to Alfie, who just stared back, giving nothing away. 'Look, I was going to audition, but to be honest I really don't want to as I'd much rather be a stage hand, and help paint the scenery and things. And anyway, I wouldn't want to be the next to audition after Arabella's performance.'

Arabella looked at me crossly for a moment, then her freckly face broke into a grin. She nodded in agreement.

'What's your name, kid?' Alfie said, reaching down for a clipboard and pen. He wrote my name under "Stage hands", then Arabella and I raced back up to our dorm while one of the twins, Moira, climbed on to the stage to say her piece.

After dancing round the room all evening yesterday, Arabella had a total mood crash this morning and is now lying under her duvet with her face in the pillow, really worried that she messed up her audition. NOTHING I say seems to make her feel better, not even the offer of one of my dark, cherry chocolates that Carrie sent. Oh I DO hope she gets a good part. Stephania said the character list should be going up later today. SO nerve wracking.com...

Friday 5th November

A bitter-sweet success, Diary.

Well, there's good news and bad news. The good news, well fabulous news, is that Arabella has been given one of the main parts – hurrah! The bad news is that she has to act opposite Clarice, who's also been given a main part. And guess what – they have to act being in love with each other! It would almost be funny if Arabella wasn't so utterly MAD about it. Arabella is going to play Hermia and Clarice is going to play the boy's role of Lysander, because we don't have any boys at our school to take those parts. Another bit of good news is that I've been made the head stage hand, which I'm really very pleased about because I can concentrate on painting the backdrops without worrying about lots of people staring at me on opening night, which would be TOO freaky for words.com.

Melody, the twins and Hannah all have main parts too. Lottie is a stage hand, and Erica didn't bother auditioning for anything, lazy thing. Cleo has a small part in the play, apparently she's going to be a wall, which I'm sure she'll be very good at because sometimes, trying to get through to her IS like talking to a brick wall. Good casting.com.

Right, I'm going to take Arabella to the school farm to calm her down. She always likes spending time with our chickens, Lemony and Superchick and anyway, it's their feeding time. She's just thrown her pillows on the floor and is sitting crossed legged on her bed, repeating, 'Why does it have to be Clarice? Why oh why oh why?'

Saturday 6th November

I can't believe it, Diary, there's been a crime!

Yesterday afternoon me and Arabella were sitting on a bale of straw in the school farm, Lemony was on my knee and Superchick was on her shoulder. We'd just cleaned out their run and Arabella was looking a lot happier.

'It's not *that* bad is it, Clarice playing opposite me? I mean, at least I got a main part, Alfie and Stephania must have thought my acting was sort of OK.' Phew, I thought. Her mood is picking up.

'Sort of OK?' I said. 'For goodness sake, Arabella, you were AMAZING, like a proper professional actress. You actually became someone else before my very eyes, it was magic.' She grinned at me. 'And yes, you're right,' I went on. 'You *should* concentrate on what a great acting role you've been given, and ignore Clarice if she acts like a rude idiot towards you. But to be honest, her acting wasn't bad either. Maybe you'll even enjoy working together.'

'Hmph.' Was all Arabella said in reply.

I lifted Lemony off my knee and was putting her on the floor for a bit of a run around, when the barn door crashed open and Melody ran in.

'Have you heard?' She panted.

'Heard what?' I said.

'There's been a theft. Apparently Moira and Lynne's dorm was ransacked yesterday during the auditions, and some of the treasure their father brought them back from his Rainforest expedition has been stolen.' Melody stopped for breath. 'They're both really upset about it.'

'What?' Me and Arabella said together.

'It's true,' Melody panted. 'I just heard Mrs Pumpernickle telling a sixth former all about it.'

'Well I'm not surprised Moira and Lynne are upset,' Arabella said. 'Their father brought them back bracelets set with rare Amazonian stones. Who on *earth* could have done such a thing?'

'I don't know,' Melody said, sitting down on another straw bale. 'But Mrs Pumpernickle is FURIOUS, and is off to have a meeting with Mrs Fairchild about it now. Moira said that their room had been completely turned over and messed up, drawers and clothes on the floor, shampoo squirted in the bath, make up all over the mirror, empty jewellery box on the floor. It was obviously someone really horrible doing it, who wanted to badly upset them.'

'Yes,' I said, flicking a long brown strand out of my face. 'What an utterly beastly thing to do. The twins are so nice, I can't imagine them having any enemies at all. Oh, I can't *bear* to think of anyone we know doing such a terrible thing. Even Cleo and Clarice wouldn't stoop that low, would they?'

'I wouldn't think so,' Melody said, rubbing her forehead. 'Actually, since they found out they've been going round putting all sorts of theories forward about who they think the thief is.'

'Hmm,' I said. 'I can just imagine, and knowing those two I bet they're not very polite theories either.'

Oh diary, a crook is in our midst. But WHO could it be? Unsettling times.com.

Sunday 7th November

Oh dear, Diary.

I have to tell you that there was a bit of drama at dinner last night. Me, Arabella, Lottie and Melody were all sitting round a table eating duck and kiwi fruit pate and crackers, when who should turn up next to our table but the lovely Cleo and Clarice. Cleo cleared her throat loudly, making sure lots of people looked up to see what was going on, before saying at the top of her voice,

'Clarice and I know who the thief is. We know who stole the twins' jewellery. We've worked it out, and we're one hundred percent sure we're right.'

She paused for dramatic effect. By now, there was quiet across the dining hall. Everyone in the school had heard about the theft and were very shocked, because things like that just didn't happen to pupils here, or so we'd thought.

'Yes,' Clarice went on. 'The thief MUST be the poor girl, Lottie Greenwood. Think about it, there were never any thefts before she arrived and she's the only poor girl at the school who can't afford to buy jewellery of her own. She must have become jealous, seeing all of our riches and wealth, and decided to steal some bracelets for herself. She wasn't even in the Grand Hall during the auditions yesterday, I remember. She asked Melody to put her name down on the 'stage hand' list.' Clarice stepped back, staring at Lottie, arms folded.

Lottie's face crumpled and she gave a big sob.

'I asked Melody to put my name down because I was too shy to come into the Grand Hall and speak to two famous celebrities. I was in my dorm the whole time, writing a letter to my mum about how I was finally starting to enjoy it here.' Another big sob. 'Oh I would never steal from anyone. Never!' And with that she jumped up and ran out of the dining hall.

'You ABSOLUTE PIGS!' Arabella jumped out of her chair and ran towards the two snobs with her fists whirring like windmills in front of her. I also jumped up and caught my friend in my arms just as she was about to whack Clarice.

'Calm down,' I whispered. 'They're not worth getting into trouble for.'

'What's all this fuss?' Mrs Pumpernickle came bustling towards us through the throng. Most girls in the room had climbed on to their chairs to get a better view, delicious dinners forgotten. Even little Polly was standing on her chair at the back of the room.

'How dare you accuse Lottie, just because she's a scholarship girl,' Arabella said, trembling with rage. 'You and your snobbish ways disgust me.'

'It was an unfair, unkind thing to do,' I agreed, looking from Cleo to Clarice while holding Arabella tightly in case she tried another attack. 'Poor Lottie, just because she's here on a scholarship it doesn't mean she's a thief, or is jealous of our things.'

'Cleo, Clarice? What have you done?' Mrs Pumpernickle demanded, now standing next to me, slightly out of breath. She looked from Arabella to the two blonde haired girls and back again.

'Oh, just telling a few home truths,' Cleo simpered, before spinning round in her high heeled shoes and strutting off, followed by Clarice. Mrs Pumpernickle looked around at everyone, eyes narrowed, clearly confused and suspicious. No one wanted to tell her about the horrible accusations so we all kept quiet.

'Right. The pantomime is *over*,' she said after a few moments, shaking her head. 'I hope whatever happened is now finished and forgotten. Sit down, act like ladies and get on with your dinners. Honestly, sometimes you'd think we were in a zoo not a boarding school, the way you lot carry on.'

Poor Lottie, being shamed in public like that. We couldn't find her ANYWHERE after dinner, I hope she's OK. I don't believe for one minute that she's the thief, but what if Cleo and Clarice have sowed a seed of doubt in people's minds with their stupid speech? That would be *too* awful. If you ask me, Erica is much more of a likely candidate, she just doesn't seem to like anyone or join in with anything.

Arabella and I had a long chat about it when we got back to our dorm. Arabella was still upset about seeing Lottie so UNFAIRLY treated, and to be honest so was I. She's new and such a sweet little thing, it was just so mean.com. We both VOWED to find the real culprit and to clear Lottie's name. She doesn't seem to have enough confidence to do that by herself, and it would be AWFUL if she decided to leave Egmont because of those two bullies. So we'll have to do some serious detecting work and sniff out the real crook. This might be difficult in between rehearsals but we'll give it our best shot.

I'm going to sleep now, tomorrow's going to be busy as Alfie and Stephania are going to talk us through the whole play. Ooh, I hope they don't argue like Mrs Fairchild said they used to...

Anyway, night night, Zzzzzzzzzzzzzzzz...

Tuesday 9th November

To be suspicious or not to be, Diary, that is the question.

Yesterday was very interesting indeed. In the morning, Arabella and I went along to the Grand Hall two minutes after nine o'clock, and found it full of all the first years from Sapphire, Emerald and Ruby classes. Alfie was pacing up and down the stage.

'You're late,' he shouted as we came in. 'Sit down.' Honestly, how impatient. It's not *my* fault my electric tooth brush fell off the bathroom shelf and splattered water on my top so that I had to change it at the last minute, is it?

We went down to the third row from the front and found places near Melody and the twins. I saw Lottie sitting next to Erica at the back, looking very pale. Just looking at her sad face made me RE-VOW to myself that I would clear her name, if I could. Erica was chewing gum, blowing big bubbles that splattered all over her face with a SNAP.

'Good morning first years,' Stephania stepped out on to the stage, looking all glowy and fresh. Today her hair was twirled into two buns that looked like twirly pastries on the sides of her head and she was wearing a soft pink tunic over grey leggings. 'Congratulations to you all for auditioning and for being given your parts. There is a wealth of talent amongst you, and our job is to draw it all together for a mind blowing performance of William Shakespeare's play, "A Midsummer Night's Dream". Everyone's role is important, the actresses *and* the stagehands, who'll also be designing the scenery. We must work together as a team to make this play a success.

Now I have one important announcement to make before we get started. Unfortunately Mrs De Nero slipped on a wet patch of moss last night as she and the music teacher, Mr Violette, walked from the minibus to the main school in the rain. The hospital phoned Mrs Fairchild this morning to confirm that Mrs De Nero's leg is badly broken, so she will be unable to help with the school play from now on. We'll all have to work extra hard to make her proud.'

There were exclamations around the hall, everyone liked Mrs De Nero and her floaty butterfly ways.

'Enough of the jibber jabber,' Alfie strutted on to the stage. He came up to Stephania's elbow. 'Let's get started.' Stephania shot him a dirty look.

'Who can tell me anything about "A Midsummer Night's Dream"?' He growled. Melody's hand shot up.

'I've been reading about it on the internet,' she said eagerly. 'It's a comedy and it's set in Greece. Basically, it's about falling in love. There are four young people and a group of actors, as well as some woodland fairies and a duchess and duke. As the character Lysander says, "The course of true love never did run smooth", and they have all sorts of adventures and complications and end up looking rather silly.'

'Wow you really have done your homework,' Stephania said, looking impressed.

'Well that's a short summary,' Alfie said, not looking pleased. 'You haven't really gone into any detail about the character's motivations. I can-'

'Yes you can tell us all about it Mr Clever Cloggs,' Stephania grinned. 'But I thought Melody did really well. We will need to tell you all about the plot in more detail as we go along, but to get into the spirit of the play, let's have a read through now.'

'Are you questioning my decision?' Alfie said, going purple. 'Do you know who I am? I'm the famous one here, not you. You only work on a television talent show for goodness sake. I'm Hollywood royalty. Just look at my entourage, then you'll realise how successful I am.'

Everyone, including Stephania, looked around at Alfie's 'people', who littered the Grand Hall, doing things like warming his socks on a radiator, brewing him a coffee on his portable coffee machine, unrolling his yoga mat and getting his face powder ready in case his nose went shiny.

'Well I'm a big girl now,' Stephania said, her grin turning cat-like. 'I don't need people to hold my hand and warm my socks for me. I think it's because I actually grew up, unlike some people around here.'

Whoa, I thought. One of their famous arguments is coming on. Cleo and Clarice had gone to stand next to Alfie defensively, pushed there by Mrs Blinkham who had brought some fairy costumes to sew while she watched the rehearsal. I thought Polly must be running around the top rows of seats unattended. Come to think of it, there was no sign of Erica or Lottie anymore. Oh dear oh dear, they must have slipped out unnoticed. I do hope there are no more robberies...

'I did not come here to be insulted,' Alfie shouted. 'Especially not by an F-list "celebrity" such as yourself. Marcus, I'm feeling stressed, bring my massage oil and let's get out of here. I can't work under these conditions.'

'Coming Alfie,' a young man with gelled black hair said, grabbing an enormous bottle of oil from a trolley before running after Alfie who was striding across the stage towards the wings. (That's a theatrical term Melody told me for the sides of the stage.) Within minutes, Alfie and his entourage had left the building, leaving us first years standing there with our mouths open and Stephania looking slightly less together than usual.

'Well I didn't expect him to actually *leave*,' she said, shuffling her script. Mrs Blinkham shot her a poisonous glance. 'What a baby. Oh well, let's get on with the rehearsal. Right, the play opens with Hermia refusing to obey her dad's wish that she marries Demetrius, so come on Arabella and Lynne, you're up first. Grab a script and let's get reading. By the way, I want you all to take your scripts away with you today, so you can start learning your lines.'

After that the rehearsal went pretty smoothly, even if the famous Hollywood director that Mrs Fairchild hired especially for the play was absent! Oh well, I couldn't help thinking Stephania quite enjoyed having a dig at him, but I couldn't work out why that might be. Honestly, adults are too confusing for words.com.

Right I'm off to meet Arabella for lunch and we're going to discuss thief-finding tactics, we've had a few ideas already...

Wednesday 10th November

Oh no Diary, worst news!

There's been another theft. This time it was Maya and Aretha from Ruby class who had their dorm looted. They came running into the dining hall yesterday during high tea, just after Arabella, Lottie and I had sat down with a plate of cherry scones, clotted cream and plum jam. We were trying to cheer Lottie up, she's hardly touched her food since being accused of stealing.

'We've been robbed,' Maya burst out. I like her, she's really good at singing and has been given the part of Titania, Queen of the Fairies, in the play.

'Our room is a TOTAL mess,' Aretha said, arriving next to Maya. She's playing the part of the Duke of Athens. 'And our purses have been emptied and the platinum necklace my grandmother gave me is missing.' She burst into tears. Maya hugged her.

'And my ring collection is gone,' Maya said, her lip wobbling. 'The pot's still there but the rings are missing, they took me years to collect and I managed to find some really unusual ones.'

'Look, we're not being rude, Lottie,' Aretha said, giving a little sob and coming over to our table. 'But if what Cleo and Clarice said the other day is true and you have taken our stuff because you can't afford your own, please could we have it back? We wouldn't blame you or anything, it's just that it's really special to us. The thing is, we noticed you weren't at the rehearsal again this afternoon.'

'But it WASN'T ME,' Lottie cried in a sort of strangled way. 'I wasn't at the rehearsal because I went to see Mrs Fairchild to ask if she could send me home. Scholarship or no scholarship, I don't want to be anywhere that I'm accused of being a thief. Ask her if you don't believe me. Oh this is all so awful.' She pushed her chair back and ran out of the dining hall.

'But Erica wasn't at the rehearsal today or at the one yesterday either,' Arabella whispered. 'I think we need to do some serious detecting.'

'Me too,' I whispered back, watching Mrs Pumpernickle put her arms round Maya and Athena before leading them off. 'I simply couldn't BEAR it if Lottie was bullied into leaving. Right, I've got an idea.'

Thursday 11th November

How unexpected.com, Diary!

So yesterday afternoon, Arabella and I skipped the rehearsal and followed Erica, to see what she did while everyone else was in the Grand Hall. Lottie had gone to sit with Mrs Fairchild again, too upset to face anybody. It was a bit of a shame because Alfie had got over his tantrum and returned to the rehearsal yesterday and I have to admit he's rather good at what he does, and really pulled everyone's acting together. We gave Melody a note to give to him, explaining that we couldn't come as we had a job to do.

'I hope we don't get caught,' I said as we positioned ourselves behind bushes near the door to the Grand Hall. I'd noticed a pattern, Erica seemed to arrive for the BEGINNING of the rehearsal, blow bubbles loudly and annoyingly, then slip out unnoticed once everyone became absorbed in the play.

'Or more likely WE'LL catch someone: the thief,' Arabella said grimly.

We waited for about ten minutes, all wrapped up in our cashmere scarves and big puffy jackets. The weather was getting colder and Mrs Pumpernickle said she thought it might snow soon.

One half of the giant door creaked open and Erica tiptoed out.

I waggled my eyebrows at Arabella and we sneaked after her, darting from bush, to statue, to fence, holding our breaths and hoping she wouldn't see us.

To my surprise, instead of heading back into the main school building where all the dorms are, Erica headed round the *side* of the school and through the kitchen garden, where Marcel grows his fruits, vegetables and herbs for cooking. She walked straight through the gate at the end and into the Japanese Rock Garden. The one good thing about the route she chose was the amount of things we could hide behind on the way, like sheds, trellises, boulders and trees. But I was completely mystified.com about where she was heading.

We dodged through the rock garden, almost being discovered when she dropped her hankie and turned to pick it up. Luckily we had just enough time to drop behind a mountain of stone before she saw us. We watched her push open the gate and walk through it to the Medieval garden. By now we were a very long way from the main building and by the looks of it, the only ones out in the freezing air.

Arabella and I stayed just behind the gate, peering through the gaps in a nearby hedge to see what Erica would do next. To my UTTER surprise.com, she pulled her fur coat round herself tightly and sat down on a bench near a fountain. Then she took the gum out of her mouth, wrapped it in a tissue, put it in her pocket, and began to sing.

Sweet, sad notes filled the air and wrapped themselves round Arabella and I. A tear rolled down Arabella's cheek and on to the grass and I found my own eyes were also a bit weepy. What a beautiful voice, but the song was full of such loneliness and passion, it went straight to my heart and made it hurt.

'Wowzers,' whispered Arabella. I nodded. At that moment, I felt like we were intruding on something very private; after all Erica had taken great pains to be away from everyone. Maybe she came here every day while were rehearsing. It seemed unlikely now that she was the thief. I wondered what was making her so sad.

'Hey Arabella,' I whispered, shifting position. 'I've got an idea. Why don't we go and get Stephania and ask her to listen to Erica sing. After all, she's the singing coach and with a voice like that Erica should be in the play. Maybe she's shy about singing in front of other people or something.'

Arabella gave me the thumbs up, so we crept back through the gardens as quietly as we could and slipped into the Grand Hall, only to get shouted at by Alfie for having commitment issues about the play. But Arabella said we needed to speak to Stephania about an important, private matter and very soon we were tiptoeing back to the Medieval garden with Stephania in tow.

Tears gushed down her cheeks as she listened to Erica sing.

'I haven't heard natural talent like this for a long time,' she whispered, wiping her eyes. 'But it's such a melancholy song. Why is she so sad?'

We both shrugged, shaking our heads. We simply had no idea. I was starting to feel a bit bad for just writing Erica off as rude and arrogant, although to be fair that IS how she'd seemed.

'I can't bear it any longer, I'm going to go and talk to her,' Stephania said. You two go and join the rehearsal now please, and thank you for alerting me to Erica and her gift.'

'Goodness,' I whispered to Arabella on the way back. 'I wonder what Erica's going to say to her.'

Friday 12th November

Mysterious events, Diary...

Erica didn't tell us or her roommate Lottie about what happened in the Medieval garden, but from that afternoon on, something seemed to change in her. For a start, she stopped going on about how silly things were at Egmont and also stopped blowing bubbles with her annoying gum. She actually gave me a half smile at dinner yesterday, which was a relief because I'd been worrying in case she was angry that we told Stephania about her singing, and was also feeling rather guilty because we'd presumed she was the thief without any real evidence.

When I met up with Lottie in the library yesterday evening so we could do our Maths homework together, she told me that Erica was being much nicer now and had confided in her about how she hadn't wanted to come to Egmont but that her father had insisted, saying that he and her mother didn't have time to look after her anymore now that his business was going global. Her feelings had been really hurt and she'd decided to hate everyone here. But apparently Stephania got on really well with her and is going to give her a singing part in the play.

'I didn't know there were any singing parts?' I said, trying to remember the script.

'Well there aren't really, but Stephania's invented some songs for a few of the fairies and elves to sing. I think she wants the girls with great voices to have a chance to show off their talents.' Lottie said. She was looking a bit better, less pale.

'Perfect for Erica then,' I smiled.

'Yes but apparently Alfie's mad about it,' Lottie chuckled. 'Says it ruins the purity of the script, or something.'

The doors to the library swung open and Amy from Emerald class burst in.

'I've been robbed,' she wailed. 'Me and Poppy went straight to our riding lesson after the rehearsal this afternoon and we only got back to our dorm five minutes ago. It's a tip and my collection of pearls is missing and Poppy's golden necklace has gone too. What shall I do?'

'Come on, let's go and find Mrs Pumpernickle,' I said, jumping up and putting my arm round Amy. 'She'll know what to do.' Lottie ran past us before we'd even gone through the library doors. I stared after her feeling really worried. She hadn't been in the rehearsal again and at this rate she wasn't going to know what props to bring on and off the stage at the right times. I'd started painting the scenery this afternoon, but could really have done with some help. Where on earth was she going every day, surely not to Mrs Fairchild's office every time? What if we'd been wrong about her? I couldn't BEAR to have that thought even once...

Sunday 14th November

A disappearance, Diary!

The plot thickened yesterday, that's for sure, and I'm not just talking about the school play. After hearing about the most recent theft, Cleo and Clarice tried to find Lottie to question her about it and no doubt bully her. But they couldn't find her anywhere.

Good for her, I thought at first, feeling bad about doubting my new friend, even for a second. Arabella and I tried to find Lottie before the afternoon's rehearsal but she'd simply vanished. Even Erica had no idea where she was, and seemed quite concerned.

'She usually comes back to our room when she's upset about something, to phone her mum, or to write her a letter or an email,' she said. 'But she didn't come back on Friday evening at all. I was so worried I went to ask Matron if Lottie was sick and had been taken into the infirmary, but she said she hadn't.'

'How odd,' I said, twiddling my plait round my finger, while trying to think about where on earth she could be. 'I *do* hope she hasn't run away.'

'I think we should go and tell Mrs Fairchild,' Arabella said. 'If something has happened to Lottie she should know, so that she can call the police to look for her if it turns out she has run away.'

Arabella, Erica and I went and knocked on Mrs Fairchild's door, making Arabella late for a costume fitting with Mrs Blinkham, which she said she didn't mind a bit as last time she was sure Mrs Blinkham had stuck pins in her on purpose.

Mrs Fairchild was listening to a CD of chimpanzee noises while doing yoga on her round mat when we went into her study.

'The lotus is always the most difficult to achieve, don't you think?' she asked. We all nodded, not knowing what to say. I was wondering how on earth her legs were so bendy.

'Well it's lovely to see you all my darlings,' She said, standing up gracefully before going to her kitchenette and switching the kettle on. 'And to what do I owe this pleasure?'

'I'm…er…afraid we've got some bad news,' Arabella said. As soon as she said that I felt like what we were going to say sounded really stupid.com, but it was too late to back out.

'Oh yes?' Mrs Fairchild did some ballet moves while she waited for the kettle to boil. 'Nothing fatal, I hope?'

'Erm, no,' I said, while Erica fiddled with her bag. 'It's just that Lottie Greenwood seems to have disappeared.'

'Gracious,' Mrs Fairchild said as she poured tea for everyone. I didn't think she looked shocked or surprised at all. 'That is, indeed, unusual news.'

'Yes it is,' Arabella said. 'And we think her disappearance is connected with these robberies. It seems no one's stuff is safe anymore, and Clarice and Cleo have been blaming Lottie for it so publically, and-'

'Yes,' Mrs Fairchild's sparkly eyes darkened. 'They have, haven't they. Possibly an unwise choice of action, to blame a new girl without any proof, don't you think?'

'Yes absolutely,' I said. 'We've stood up for Lottie from the start, it's just that she's never at rehearsals and now she's gone missing, and um...do you think she might have run away?'

'It wouldn't surprise me at all if she felt like running away,' Mrs Fairchild's eyes still hadn't got back their sparkle. 'How would you feel as a new girl who hasn't had the same material privileges as the rest of the school, to be named, shamed and blamed so soon after arriving, for a crime you most probably did not commit?'

'I think we'd all feel awful,' Arabella said, hanging her head and me and Erica nodded. My heart fell into my feet, thinking about how TERRIBLE and sad Lottie must have felt to have the whole school doubting her.

'But where is she?' I said. 'If only we could find her, we could somehow make her feel better.'

'That is a nice, kind thought,' Mrs Fairchild's eyes twinkled again. 'But I fear you are asking the wrong questions. Perhaps instead of asking, "Where is Lottie?" You should be saying to yourselves, "Who is the real thief and how can we catch them?" She finished her tea and stood up, walking to the door. Our meeting with her was clearly at an end.

'Blimey,' Arabella whispered, as we walked away from her study. 'She seemed pretty sure that Lottie wasn't the thief, and she didn't seem at all surprised to hear she was missing, did she?'

'Nope,' I said. 'I think she knows what's happened to Lottie, whatever that may be. But I think she wanted us to investigate further and find out who else might be the robber.'

'And that,' Arabella said, sighing. 'Is going to be very difficult.'

Tuesday 16th November

Still no sign of Lottie, Diary.

It's been four days now, and rumours are sweeping through the school, (probably started by Cleo and Clarice), that Lottie's been expelled for thieving. But after talking to Mrs Fairchild that just doesn't seem likely. Arabella and I have been interviewing everyone who's had things stolen, trying to see if the thief left any clues in any of the dorms but so far no one's come up with any evidence.

Now a different type of drama has occurred, and OH MY GOODNESS ME, what a drama it was.

Basically, yesterday we were all in the Grand Hall as usual, rehearsing "A Midsummer Night's Dream". I'd been painting a huge forest backdrop, putting in all sorts of shades of green to create a glade surrounded by tall evergreens. My hand was aching after all the painting so I asked Bridget and Ada from Emerald Class to take over painting the woodland creatures that peep out from behind the trees.

Arabella wasn't acting because Alfie and Stephania were coaching Cleo through Act Five, Scene One, concentrating on her part as a wall.

'Can you uncross your arms for me love?' Stephania said patiently. 'I don't think walls tend to fold their arms, do they?'

'I don't think people tend to act like walls,' Cleo snapped.

'Oh give me patience,' Alfie yelled, throwing his script on the floor. 'The girl can't even act being a wall. A wall! It's just a WALL how hard can it be.' I was with Alfie on that one, Cleo did seem to be being rather difficult.

'Now just hold two fingers up, love, at this point the wall needs to make a chink...' Stephania was saying as I slid down further in my seat and turned to Arabella. We were sitting on the back row of seats having a chat.

'I'm stumped,' I said. 'I mean really, the thief could be ANYONE that is on the school grounds, including any of the old Egmont girls. It could even be someone from Alfie's entourage, there are so many of them and one of his people could be slipping out unnoticed every day.'

'Ooh, I hadn't thought of that,' Arabella said, also sliding down in her seat and pulling a squashed bar of chocolate out of her pocket. She gave me a piece and we munched silently, watching Hannah, who plays the part of Puck, escort little Polly out of the hall, probably to the toilet.

'It could even be Marcel's new chef, Antoine,' she said, licking her fingers. 'Although he always seems very smiley. Or what about the new dinner lady?'

'Yep, could be her,' I said. 'Or how about the gardener's helper, that young man who's started coming in to help clear the leaves. Or even Cleo and Clarice trying to frame Lottie because they're such snobs?'

'Yes,' Arabella sighed. 'Could be any of them. I know, why don't we-'

There was a shriek from the stage and we shifted up to see what was going on.

'I beg your pardon?' Stephania uncrossed her long legs and stood up. She'd been sitting near Cleo in the middle of the stage, but now curled her fingers into fists and walked towards Alfie, who was standing, quivering, at the front. I think the shriek had come from him.

'I said "What a surprise",' Alfie almost screamed the words, a bit of a change from his usual gravelly tones. 'Miss Perfect Stephania is refusing to listen to common sense. AGAIN. I'm telling you, this child CANNOT ACT. I'm firing her, she's ruining the play.'

Cleo was doing the best impression of a wall she'd done all day, standing rigidly still in between the two adults, arms unfolded, only her eyes flicking from one to the other.

'She's a child, you pompous idiot, a CHILD,' Stephania screamed, towering over Alfie. I'd never seen her so het up, it made goose-bumps spring up all over my arms. 'You can't fire a child. This is not one of your million dollar, boring, Hollywood flicks. This is a SCHOOL PLAY.'

'Boring?' Alfie yelled back. 'I'll tell you what's boring, it's those low budget television game shows you make. Listen sweet-pea, I'm in charge here, not you. Although your ego clearly doesn't understand that.'

'My ego?' Stephania shouted. 'What about your gigantic, inflated sense of self? It's so big it's crowding the rest of us out of this hall.'

'Are you the director or am I?' Alfie bawled. 'Because last time I looked, Miss Smarty Pants, it was me. So why don't you just be quiet and take some direction for once?'

'I would take some direction if the director actually knew what he was talking about,' Stephania spat. 'It's like working with a two year old.'

'*I'm* the star here, NOT YOU.' Alfie looked like he was about to throw himself on the floor and have a temper tantrum. Stephania turned and walked back to the chair. She bent down and picked up her bag.

'I'm not staying here to be insulted like this,' she said. She looked round the hall. 'Sorry girls, but I resign. I can't work with this imbecile for one moment longer.' Sharp intakes of breath could be heard everywhere as we all watched Stephania turn and walk off stage left. (Melody told me that term too, it basically means right, not left, so complicated.com).

'This is a circus, not a play,' Alfie threw his script on the floor for the second time. 'I've never worked under such conditions. Never. Come on team, let's get out of here. I quit.' He stormed off stage, short legs working hard. In seconds his team of hairdressers, drink carriers and phone holders had also vanished.

'I'm not ruining the play and I *am* a good actress,' Cleo threw herself on the floor and beat her fists up and down, as Clarice and her mother ran up the steps.

'Drama queen,' Arabella whispered.

'We're doomed,' Clarice moaned as her mother patted Cleo's shoulder. 'Now I'll never be a Hollywood actress.'

I rolled my eyes and sprang up out of my seat.

'Come with me,' I pulled Arabella upright. 'I've got an idea.'

We ran down to the stage and climbed up.

'Listen,' I tried to shout above the chatter that had broken out all around the hall. 'If you just listen for a moment, I've thought of an idea.' A hush fell at the same moment that I remembered I didn't like being on a stage with people looking at me. Arabella must have sensed my fear.

'Keep going,' she grabbed my hand and squeezed it. 'You're doing a great job.'

'Um...' I said. 'Right...The thing is, I think I can step in here. You all know most of your lines and when to come on and off stage. I know you do, because as head stage hand I've been at most of the rehearsals watching. So basically, all you have to do is keep practising.' I took a deep breath, feeling a little more confident.

'Look, in a week's time it will be opening night and most of our parents, friends and relations are coming to watch. We can't let them down, so let's do our best. The show must go on! Who's with me?'

Arabella and Melody's hands shot straight up. Then so did Erica's, Lynne's and Moira's. One by one, everyone raised their hands except Cleo, Clarice and Mrs Blinkham.

'So you think you're a big shot director all of a sudden do you, Davina Dupree?' Cleo stood up, brushed herself down and sauntered towards me. 'Think you can follow in Alfie Calpone's footsteps?'

'As a matter of fact, yes Cleo, I do,' I sighed, putting my hands on my hips to try and appear stronger than I felt. 'So you can either join in or explain to Mrs Fairchild and Mrs Pumpernickle why you're the only first year sitting in the audience on opening night, with someone else, maybe even *me*, playing the part of the wall.'

Cleo shot me her filthiest look but said no more and retreated behind Clarice.

'Right everyone, are we ready?' I yelled. 'Let's start from the beginning. Positions please, lights down, let's go.'

'Wow, you're amazing. Go Davina,' Arabella whispered as she ran to her place.

I can tell you one thing, it's EXHAUSTING.COM being a director. I've been trying to think about the thief since we got back to our dorm, but... Zzzzzzzzz.....

Thursday 18th November

Utter disaster, Diary!

Arabella and I have been robbed. We'd just got back from a REALLY long day of rehearsals and were both so tired we'd planned to make our favourite hot chocolate with fudge and marshmallows as a treat. But when we walked in to our dorm, we saw UTTER CARNAGE.COM!

My duvet was on the floor and my draws had been emptied out all over my bed. The black, silk bag for my collection of precious stones that Dad had brought back from one of his secret spy missions in the pacific was there, but the stones had gone.

Arabella stomped round the dorm in a rage, checking her stuff.

'My white gold trinket box has been taken,' she thundered. 'And look, all our clothes have been thrown on the floor. Ooh I REALLY want to find whoever's done this and shake them till they-'

'Calm down,' I said, not feeling very calm myself. 'Stop kicking things around, we shouldn't disturb the crime scene until we've investigated properly. The thief may have left some sort of clue about his or hers identity.'

I picked my way through the debris, staring at the scattered possessions, trying to spot anything that didn't belong to either of us. Arabella lay on her stomach on her bed, with her feet hooked over one side as an anchor, glancing over the floor.

'Aha,' she said. 'What's that?' I looked over at where she was pointing. An orange and white, rather fancy hair clip was lying next to one of my slippers. I knew it didn't belong to me or Arabella so I picked it up and turned it over in my hands.

'Hmm, it looks familiar somehow. Do you recognise it?' I said.

'Let's see it,' Arabella said, sitting up with her hand outstretched. 'I know what you mean, I've definitely seen it somewhere before but I can't think where.'

'Well at least we know the thief is a girl now,' I said, pulling my duvet back on to my bed. Annoying thief, making me tidy up which is one of my LEAST favourite things to do. 'That narrows it down a bit, we can forget the gardener's helper, most of Alfie's entourage and Antoine the chef.'

'Yep, you're right,' Arabella said. 'And it also proves that Cleo and Clarice were wrong about Lottie being the thief. She's gone and there's been another theft. It really is a total mystery. Come on, let's go and report the robbery to Mrs Pumpernickle and then make ENORMOUS mugs of hot chocolate, we certainly deserve them now. We can leave the boring tidying up till tomorrow.'

I followed her out of the room, angry that someone had stolen our personal stuff and annoyed with myself for having suspected the wrong people as it had wasted precious culprit-catching time. Right, from now on we MUST be on the lookout for orange and white hair clip wearing people...

Saturday 20th November

From bad to worse, Diary.

I'm seriously considering cancelling the whole show. I mean, for goodness sake! I thought we were nearly ready, but it turns out I was horribly mistaken.

During the rehearsal today I realised how many people don't *really* know their lines: a lot. I also realised that since I've taken over as director, no one's been painting the scenery so there are bits of wood everywhere without even a splash of paint on them. So stressful.com. I put Bridget and Ada in charge of completing all the scenery pretty quickly, as we only have THREE DAYS LEFT UNTIL OPENING NIGHT ON THE 23rd NOVEMBER. AGH! At this rate my hair is going to go as grey as Carrie's. I phoned her before for some moral support and she told me to calm down and that everything would be OK. "You can do it, gel", she said. Then she said, "And I've already paid for me ticket to come and see the play and it was bloomin' expensive, so just you make sure it's up to scratch". No pressure then.

I also realised that Mrs Blinkham and the other mothers haven't got all the costumes ready yet! Mrs Blinkham has been concentrating on making Clarice a different costume for each scene, as well as making a wall outfit for Cleo. Poor Arabella doesn't have a dress yet, and Melody, the twins, Erica and Hannah don't have their outfits either. Oh please can someone whisk me away to a desert island so I don't have to deal with this stress? Please, like right away.com?

Sunday 21st November

A slight improvement, Diary.

The mothers sat up all night sewing, so now most of the costumes are ready. The rehearsal today wasn't too bad, Erica sang so well we all stood up to applaud her at the end. Still no sign of Alfie and Stephania, I think they're so pathetic.com for just storming off and leaving us in the lurch and I can't believe our drama teacher is out of action too. What are the chances?! I hope Mrs Fairchild's told the "celebrities" how disappointed she is. At least there have been no more burglaries, I don't think I could cope with any more of them on top of this director stress. Mrs Pumpernickle said she had a serious talk with Mrs Fairchild about the thieving, and that they're seriously thinking of calling the police in if the burglar can't be found over the next few days by Egmont girls or staff.

I don't have time to write any more today I'm afraid, Diary because I've got to go back to the Grand Hall. We're rehearsing Act Two, Scene Two, which is one of the most important in the play because it's where Puck (Hannah) makes a mistake with the love potion which starts the mass confusion between the characters. It's basically what the comedy is all about so we've got to get it RIGHT.

Also, it's the dress rehearsal tomorrow so wish me luck. Hang on a minute, it's actually supposed to be BAD luck to say GOOD luck in the theatre. Melody told me you have to say break a leg instead. (Although that sounds quite painful and Mrs De Nero's already done that so I hope no one else does.)

Monday 22nd November

Help me, Diary!

The dress rehearsal was a shambles and there's been another robbery. This time it was Cleo and Clarice's dorm that was burgled. Arabella says it serves them right for blaming Lottie. I think Mrs Fairchild will have to call the police in now, so many pieces of jewellery have been stolen and the thief is still at large. I can't believe we live in such a crime ridden school, it makes me want to hire a bodyguard.

Sorry but I can't stop to chat, I have to go and sort out Cleo who can't seem to act like a wall at the right times...OPENING NIGHT TOMORROW and I feel bad because at the moment I simply don't have the time to concentrate on finding the thief...

Tuesday 23rd November

At last we have an answer, Diary! The thief has been caught. Well sort of...

Basically, this morning, private jets and helicopters starting plopping down all over the hockey pitch, ejecting extremely expensive looking mothers and fathers all over the wet grass.

'It's starting,' I whispered to Arabella as we watched more and more people arrive from our dorm window. I hadn't been able to eat my egg and soldiers for breakfast which was EXTREMELY unlike me. 'Is it too late to cancel the play?'

'Yes of course it is and don't worry, you big silly, everything will be fine.' Arabella nudged me, although I wasn't convinced because she looked even paler than usual.

I had to go to the Grand Hall after that to check everything was ready, even though we had a few hours to go. It took a while to round up Mrs Fairchild's gardener, who'd kindly agreed to do the lighting and to get Mrs Blinkham to bring all the costumes backstage. Cleo and Clarice were already there, shovelling make up on to their faces.

'Oh look, the hot shot director's arrived,' Cleo sneered. I ignored her and checked all the props were in the right place and that the scenery was ready for the stage hands to bring on and off.

Sooner than I'd have liked, I heard the general murmur of the audience arriving. Mrs Pumpernickle came backstage to help me get everyone into their costumes. We were all standing in the largest dressing room, Mrs Blinkham adjusting Arabella's dress, when I noticed that little Polly was helping herself to a basket of props. She was stuffing paper flowers and scrolls into the enormous designer handbag she likes to lug about.

'Hey Polly,' I said. 'Please don't touch those props, we need them for our play.' Mrs Blinkham's head snapped round. Although she doesn't like disciplining her child it seems she certainly doesn't like anyone else doing it.

'Leave her alone,' she said. 'She's only playing.'

'She can play with her own toys, I'm afraid we really need those things for the start of the play.' I went over to Polly and bent down. 'Could I have a look in your bag please, so I can find my things?'

Polly grinned and shoved her bag towards me. I reached down and pulled out the scrolls that the players use and then carefully lifted out the paper flowers. As I carefully scooped up a handful of fragile petals, my hand brushed against a pile of hard metal.

'Funny toys you've got in there Polly,' I said, and opened the bag to have a look.

I nearly fainted!

'Arabella, come and take a look at this. In fact I think EVERYONE should come and have a look, especially Mrs Blinkham.'

Arabella sprinted over to have a look in the bag. At the bottom of it was a mess of priceless jewellery; bracelets mixed up with necklaces, rings stuck on top of tiaras and anklets, precious stones and pearls jumbling around a trinket box .

'So you're the thief, Polly,' Arabella breathed. Polly beamed.

'What do you mean she's the thief?' Mrs Blinkham said, marching over. 'Don't be ridiculous.' She grabbed Polly's bag and stared into it. 'Oh,' she said.

'But Mummy she *can't* be,' Clarice wailed. 'We thought Lottie was the thief but now we're pretty sure it's the new chef, Antoine-'

'No I'm afraid YOUR little sister is the culprit,' Arabella said, looking extremely cheerful. 'And I must say, she's had more than enough opportunity to run wild as your mother hardly ever even looks at her. I can't think why we didn't think of Polly before.'

'How dare you insult me,' Mrs Blinkham snarled. 'Polly dear, did someone put those pretty things in your bag?'

'I took them,' Polly said happily. 'I like shiny things.'

'She must have gone round taking them whenever she was bored at rehearsals,' I said, feeling SO relieved that Lottie's name had been cleared in front of everyone. Arabella grinned at me then looked at her watch.

'Five minutes,' she mouthed.

'Right everyone, positions please,' I said, suddenly feeling rather chilly and strange. 'And er...break a leg. Mrs Blinkham, maybe you could sort out all the jewellery and return it to the correct owners after the performance?'

Clarice's mum just stuck her nose in the air, grabbed Polly's hand and the bag of jewels and strutted off.

Clarice, Arabella and I walked to the side of the stage. The red velvet curtain was down and from the sounds of hustle and bustle behind it, we had pretty much a full house.

'Enjoy yourselves, you two. You deserve to, you've both worked really hard,' I said. Arabella grinned and Clarice gave me a half smile.

CRASH!

I peeped round the curtain in time to see Alfie Calpone and Stephania Sellwig march through the swinging Grand Hall doors and down the aisle. And guess what? They were hand in hand! They reached the stage, jumped on to it (Stephania had to pull Alfie up a bit as his legs weren't quite long enough) then marched off stage left towards where me, Arabella, Clarice and very rapidly the rest of the first years stood.

'Sorry about that guys,' Alfie said, scratching his head, his cheeks flushing pink. 'Stephie and I just had a few artistic differences to sort out.'

'Looks like you're the best of friends now though,' Arabella said, staring at their hands.

'Something rather wonderful just happened,' Stephania said, looking all dreamy. 'You see, just after we had that awful argument in front of you, which I'm very sorry about, I grabbed my bike and pedalled up the drive. I was so angry with Alfie for being arrogant and rude.'

'And I was angry because Stephie was being stubborn and obstinate,' Alfie said. 'So my team and I jumped into our cars and drove off. But who should we pass pedalling furiously up the steep drive, but this fine lady here. I took one look at her and thought to myself, "Alfie, maybe she was right, maybe you were acting like a two year old in there. It's time to act like a grown up now and sort this disagreement out".'

'So he wound down his window and asked if I'd like to go to a restaurant with him to smooth out our differences. He said we owed it to you lot because you'd worked so hard on the play.'

'She agreed, and a couple of days later we met up in a restaurant in Little Pineham, a village not far from here,' Alfie went on. 'We sat at that table for six hours, just talking.'

'And after about two hours we both realised we didn't *dislike* each other at all,' Stephania said, smiling at Alfie, who winked back.

'Yep,' Alfie said. 'In fact, we realised, almost at the same time, that we're two halves of the same whole. We balance each other out. It's like we're meant to be together.'

'Opposites attract,' Stephania said, resting her chin on Alfie's head.

'Ooh, it's just like in "A Midsummer Night's Dream",' Melody squealed. 'You two are so different from each other, like the characters in the play, and your story is so unbelievable it makes me feel like I'm in a dream. Maybe WE are the ridiculous, clumsy players, contrasting with your love story.'

'Hmm, speak for yourself,' Clarice said.

I realised my mouth was hanging open like a goldfish's, so I shut it and looked at my watch.

'I'm truly flabbergasted by your news,' I said to Stephania and Alfie. 'And I'm so glad you came back, even if it is at the last minute.' They hung their heads, looking miserable. 'And now I don't mean to be rude, but the curtain's going up in one minute.'

'In that case, break a leg everybody,' Alfie said, actually SMILING round at us. 'You'll make us proud, I know you will.'

'Why do people keep telling me to break my leg?' Came Cleo's voice from the other side of the stage.

Later that evening, Tuesday 23rd November

The play was an absolute ROARING success, Diary!

I'm pleased to report that no one forgot any of their lines, and the audience oohed and aahed when Erica sang. Honestly, she's like a different girl now.

It was a *bit* embarrassing when Carrie opened her bag of crisps and sucked on her box drink during a quiet bit, I stuck my head round the curtain to see what the noise was then quickly wished I hadn't because Carrie stood up and waved! Rather mortifying.com. But to be honest it was so good to see her enjoying herself that I didn't mind too much.

We got three standing ovations where the audience stood up and clapped and called for more, so Hannah had to do Puck's end speech again and again. At the very end Alfie and Stephania appeared on stage and called me out. I didn't want to go because there were too many people watching, so Arabella came and took my hand and literally DRAGGED me out of the wings.

'We just wanted to say a special thank you to Davina Dupree, for stepping into the role of director while Stephania and I were, er…discussing our artistic differences,' Alfie said. 'As you just saw, she did a great job with the production, for which we will always be grateful.' He gave me such a hard pat on the back I almost flew into the audience.

I felt the skin on my face prickle rather deliciously as Stephania produced an ENORMOUS bunch of flowers from behind her back and gave them to me, kissing me on both cheeks.

'And if it wasn't for Davina holding the fort, Alfie and I may never have had time to come to an important decision,' she said, her cheeks glowing.

'I've asked Stephie to be my wife and she's accepted,' Alfie's face cracked into an unexpected smile.

'We're getting married next year,' Stephania said, beaming. 'And of course, all the first years are invited.'

A big cheer erupted around the hall. The only person I saw not listening was Mrs Blinkham, who was sorting out jewellery into piles, with the BIGGEST frown on her face.

After the excitement was over and we'd given Carrie a backstage tour while her taxi driver listened to the radio, (am seriously considering becoming a director when I grow up), Arabella and I tidied up the props, putting the paper flowers and scrolls back in their basket. Just as we'd collected the last few, a dark brown haired girl opened the Grand Hall doors.

'Lottie!' I shouted. 'Come here and let me HUG YOU.'

In a few seconds I'd wrapped my arms round Lottie's tiny body and lifted her off the ground. She patted my back, laughing.

'Put me down, you idiot,' she said, so I did.

'Where on *earth* have YOU been?' Arabella came striding over and gave Lottie another bear hug. 'We were worried about you.'

'Well you probably won't believe it, but I've been hiding out in Mrs Fairchild's luxury penthouse apartment, at the top of the school,' Lottie grinned. 'She was at the play this evening and told me all about Polly being the thief, so I came straight to find you.

I was spending most of my spare time with her anyway, at first because I was so homesick, and then later because everyone thought I was the thief. She knew it couldn't have been me because I spent so much time with her, so she decided to protect me.'

'Wow,' Arabella and I said together.

'I told her to send me home because I obviously didn't belong in a school like Egmont if people were going to presume I did bad things just because I didn't have as much money as them, but she told me she wouldn't hear of it. She said it would be good for certain Egmont girls to realise that it's what you are inside that matters, not how many possessions you have,' Lottie said. I felt my cheeks burn as I remembered my moment of doubt for Lottie.

'That day in the library,' Lottie went on. 'When Amy burst in to say that she and Poppy had been robbed, I saw a flicker of doubt in your eyes, Davina. That was the last straw for me, I simply couldn't bear knowing that even my new friends thought I was the thief. So that's the point Mrs

Fairchild told me to pack my things and come and stay in her apartment.'

'I'm *so sorry*, Lottie,' I said, feeling TERRIBLE. 'I didn't really suspect you, it's just that at that point I didn't know what to think, everything just seemed so confusing, and-'

'Let's never say another word about it,' Lottie said, looking more confident than I'd ever seen her. 'The most important thing is that you both stood up to Cleo and Clarice for me when they first accused me, and I'll never forget that kindness.'

After Lottie had gone, saying she and Erica were going swimming together, (I think those two will soon be best friends), Arabella and I walked back to our dorm, tired but happy.

I saw the glittery pink envelopes on our beds as soon as I opened the door.

'Look, Arabella, what on earth are these?' I asked, picking mine up straight up and ripping it open. As I read its contents, my eyebrows grew higher and higher...

To the dear first years,

Your geography teacher, Mr Fossil, and I have organised a compulsory school trip for you all.

At the beginning of next term we will travel together in private jets to the Beach of Golden Sands, about fifty miles away from Egmont, where a private yacht will be waiting to sail us to Ni Island, a little known sand island where hundreds of rare bird and animal species live.

We will all live there in luxury tents for ten days, to give you the chance of studying the wildlife under Mr Fossil's tuition. I must tell you that pirates were spotted sailing close to Ni Island a few years ago, but I have been assured by the Department of the Seven Seas that they have all since been captured and imprisoned. I shall be writing to reassure your parents and guardians of the safety and educational value of the trip this evening,

Always yours truly,

Mrs Fairchild

Made in the USA
Lexington, KY
04 June 2019